SESAME STREET

ABBY CADABBY'S
Rhyme Time

By P.J. Shaw
Illustrated by Tom Leigh

Dalmatian
Press

Dalmatian Press, 2007. All rights reserved. Printed in the U.S.A. 1-866-418-2572
The DALMATIAN PRESS name and logo are trademarks of Dalmatian Publishing Group, LLC, Franklin, Tennessee 37067.
No part of this book may be reproduced or copied in any form without written permission from the copyright owner.

Printed in the U.S.A.
ISBN: 1-40374-196-4 (M) 1-40373-609 (X)

08 09 10 11 BM 10 9 8 7 6 5 4 3
16234 Sesame Street 8x8 Storybook: Abby Cadabby's Rhyme Time

"Lumpkin, bumpkin, diddle-diddle dumpkin, zumpkin, frumpkin, pumpkin!

As a fairy-in-training, I practice my magic tricks with rhymes—you know, words that end with the same sound, like **bat** and **cat**! Rhymes are so fun to find! I know—let's find some rhymes together. Hmmmm. What words rhyme with … **rhyme**?"

What words rhyme with **sheep**?
Noisy cars that go "**beep**"!
A ballet dancer's **leap**,
And a trash heap to **sweep**.

What words rhyme with **go**?
I bet that you **know**!
There's a boat you can **row**,
And cars that go *slooooow*.

What rhymes with **icky**?
Bubblegum that is **sticky**,
A game that is **tricky**,
And dogs who are **licky**.

Which words sound like **zap**?
Fairy wings going **flap**!
And the shoes that you **tap**
To the beat—as you **snap**!

Do some words rhyme with **stick**?
Yes! A house made of **brick**,
A soft baby **chick**,
Or a camera to **click**!

What rhymes with **tub**?
Well, there's **scrub-a-dub-dub**,
And a miniature **sub**,
Or one baby bear **cub**!

What rhymes with **nose**?
Snuffleupagus **toes**,
A swishy fish that **glows**!
And a slithery **hose**.

What words rhyme with **sloppy**,
Like Oscar's **Jalopy**?
Bunnies all **hoppy**
With ears that are **floppy**.

And last, what rhymes with **tabby**?
A blankie that's **shabby**,
A fairy named **Abby**,
And the family **Cadabby**!